MCA
J
P.T.
DIVORCE ING
12.99

DISCARD

DISCARD
Schmitz

DISCARD

# Standing on My Own Two Feet

## A Child's Affirmation of Love in the Midst of Divorce

PSS!
PRICE STERN SLOAN

For Olivia, Ian, and Addison

Special thanks to Sue Diorio, Fr. Terry Hamilton, Paul Korchak,
Dave Maly, and Earl & Alma Schmitz

PRICE STERN SLOAN
Published by the Penguin Group
Penguin Group (USA) Inc., 375 Hudson Street, New York, New York 10014, USA
Penguin Group (Canada), 90 Eglinton Avenue East, Suite 700, Toronto, Ontario M4P 2Y3, Canada
(a division of Pearson Penguin Canada Inc.)
Penguin Books Ltd., 80 Strand, London WC2R 0RL, England
Penguin Group Ireland, 25 St. Stephen's Green, Dublin 2, Ireland
(a division of Penguin Books Ltd.)
Penguin Group (Australia), 250 Camberwell Road, Camberwell, Victoria 3124, Australia
(a division of Pearson Australia Group Pty. Ltd.)
Penguin Books India Pvt. Ltd., 11 Community Centre, Panchsheel Park, New Delhi—110 017, India
Penguin Group (NZ), 67 Apollo Drive, Rosedale, North Shore 0632, New Zealand
(a division of Pearson New Zealand Ltd.)
Penguin Books (South Africa) (Pty.) Ltd., 24 Sturdee Avenue,
Rosebank, Johannesburg 2196, South Africa

Penguin Books Ltd., Registered Offices: 80 Strand, London WC2R 0RL, England

The scanning, uploading, and distribution of this book via the Internet or via any other means without the permission of the publisher is illegal and punishable by law. Please purchase only authorized electronic editions and do not participate in or encourage electronic piracy of copyrighted materials. Your support of the author's rights is appreciated.

Text and illustrations copyright © 2008 by Tamara Schmitz. All rights reserved. Published by Price Stern Sloan, a division of Penguin Young Readers Group, 345 Hudson Street, New York, New York 10014. *PSS!* is a registered trademark of Penguin Group (USA) Inc. Manufactured in Singapore.

Library of Congress Control Number: 2007037014

ISBN 978-0-8431-3221-2                                        10 9 8 7 6 5 4 3 2

# Mom & Dad love

_michael Thecmok_
_wo_      name

# unconditionally.
# (No matter what!)

Mom's House

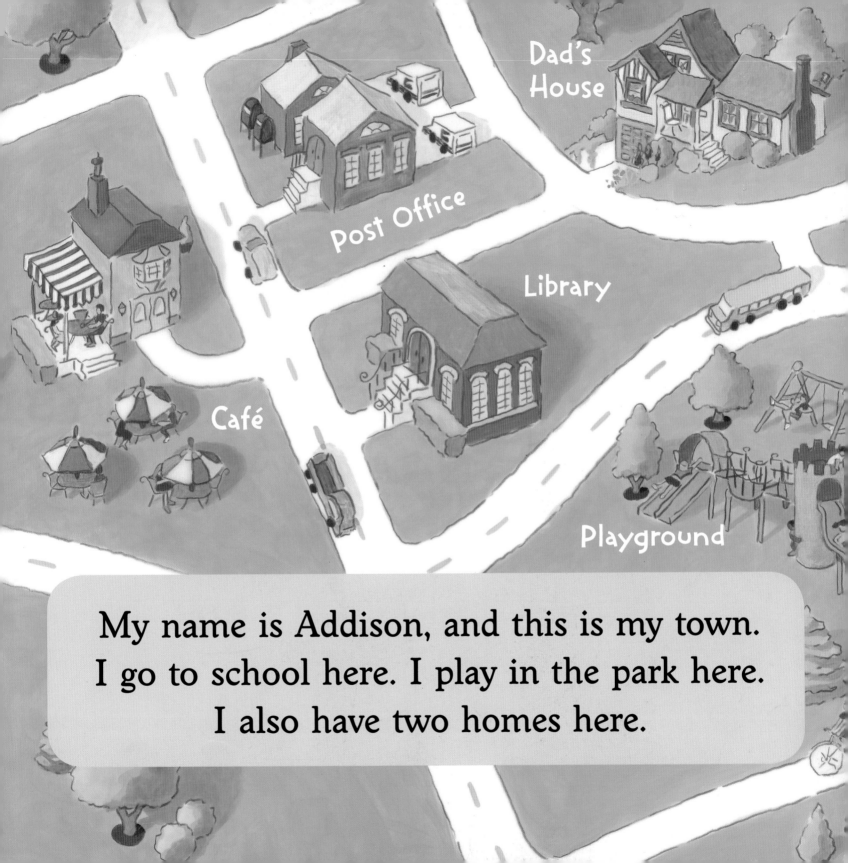

Dad's
House

Post Office

Library

Café

Playground

My name is Addison, and this is my town.
I go to school here. I play in the park here.
I also have two homes here.

This is my home at my mom's.

This is my home at my dad's.
My mom and dad are divorced.

Just like I have two feet . . .

. . . I have two homes.

I am safe at home with my mom.

I am safe at home with my dad.

Sometimes I miss the one I'm not with.

I thank my lucky stars for the phone.

Even when we
are apart, we
can look out our
windows . . .

. . . and enjoy
the same moon.

Mom
and
Dad
do not
always
get
along.

But it's not because of me.

Mom and Dad live in different homes.

But it's not because of me.

Even though I wish
we could all live
together again, that
probably won't happen.

It's not up to me.

No matter what
happens, they'll ALWAYS
be my mom and dad!

My mom loves me.

My dad loves me.

I am

loved,

and this
makes me
**strong!**

Lots of things change.

But the one thing that will never, ever,

ever,

ever,

ever,

EV

change . . .

. . . is that my mom and dad love me!

From the tippy-top of my head . . .

. . . down to my toes.